This book belongs to:

____

For Harry and Megan. G.P.

This paperback was first published in 2013 by Andersen Press Ltd.
Published in Australia by Random House Australia Pty., Level 3, 100 Pacific Highway, North Sydney, NSW 2060.
First published in Great Britain in 2012 by Andersen Press Ltd., 20 Vauxhall Bridge Road, London SW1V 2SA.

Colour separated in Switzerland by Photolitho AG, Zürich. Printed and bound in Singapore by Tien Wah Press.
Tony Ross has used pen, ink and watercolour in this book.

10 9 8 7 6 5 4 3 2 1

British Library Cataloguing in Publication Data available.
ISBN 978 1 84939 319 5

GERVASE PHINN TONY ROSS

Andersen Press

One hot, hot day in the middle of the deep, deep jungle, a strange little creature hatched out of an egg.

He scratched...

and he yawned...

and he opened his big round eyes and looked around him.

"Who am I?" he asked himself. "Where do I come from?"
Off he went plodding through the tall, **tall** grass to find out.

Soon he met a creature with a very long neck.

"Excuse me," said the strange little creature chirpily. "Could you tell me who I am and where I come from?"

"I have no idea," chuckled the creature. "I know that I am the giraffe and I am the tallest animal in the whole wide world, but I do not know what sort of creature you are."

So the strange little creature plodded on through the tall grass.

Soon he met a creature with two great tusks.

"Excuse me," said the strange little creature cheerfully. "Could you tell me who I am and where I come from?"

"I have no idea," trumpeted the creature. "I know that I am the elephant and I am the strongest animal in the whole wide world, but I do not know what sort of creature you are."

So the strange little creature plodded on through the tall grass.

Soon he met a creature with very long legs.

"Excuse me," said the strange little creature shyly. "Could you tell me who I am and where I come from?"

"I have no idea," snarled the creature. "I know that I am the cheetah and I am the fastest animal in the whole wide world, but I do not know what sort of creature you are."

So the strange little creature plodded on through the tall grass.

Soon he met a creature with a sharp, pointed horn.

"Excuse me," said the strange little creature anxiously. "Could you tell me who I am and where I come from?"

"I have no idea," snorted the creature. "I know that I am the rhinoceros and I am the toughest animal in the whole wide world, but I do not know what sort of creature you are."

So the strange little creature plodded on through the tall grass.

Soon he met a creature with a very hairy body.

"Excuse me," said the strange little creature timidly. "Could you tell me who I am and where I come from?"

"I have no idea," chattered the creature. "I know that I am the chimpanzee and I am the cleverest animal in the whole wide world, but I do not know what sort of creature you are."

So the strange little creature plodded on through the tall grass.

Soon he came to a deep, dark, muddy river and there, resting on the bank, was a creature with great yellow eyes and a wide smiling mouth.

"Excuse me," said the strange little creature desperately. "Could you tell me who I am and where I come from?"

"Yes I can," snapped the creature.

"You can!" exclaimed the strange little creature.

"I can, but you will have to come a little closer," whispered the creature, smiling and opening **wide** his jaws.

"Climb on my nose and I will tell you."

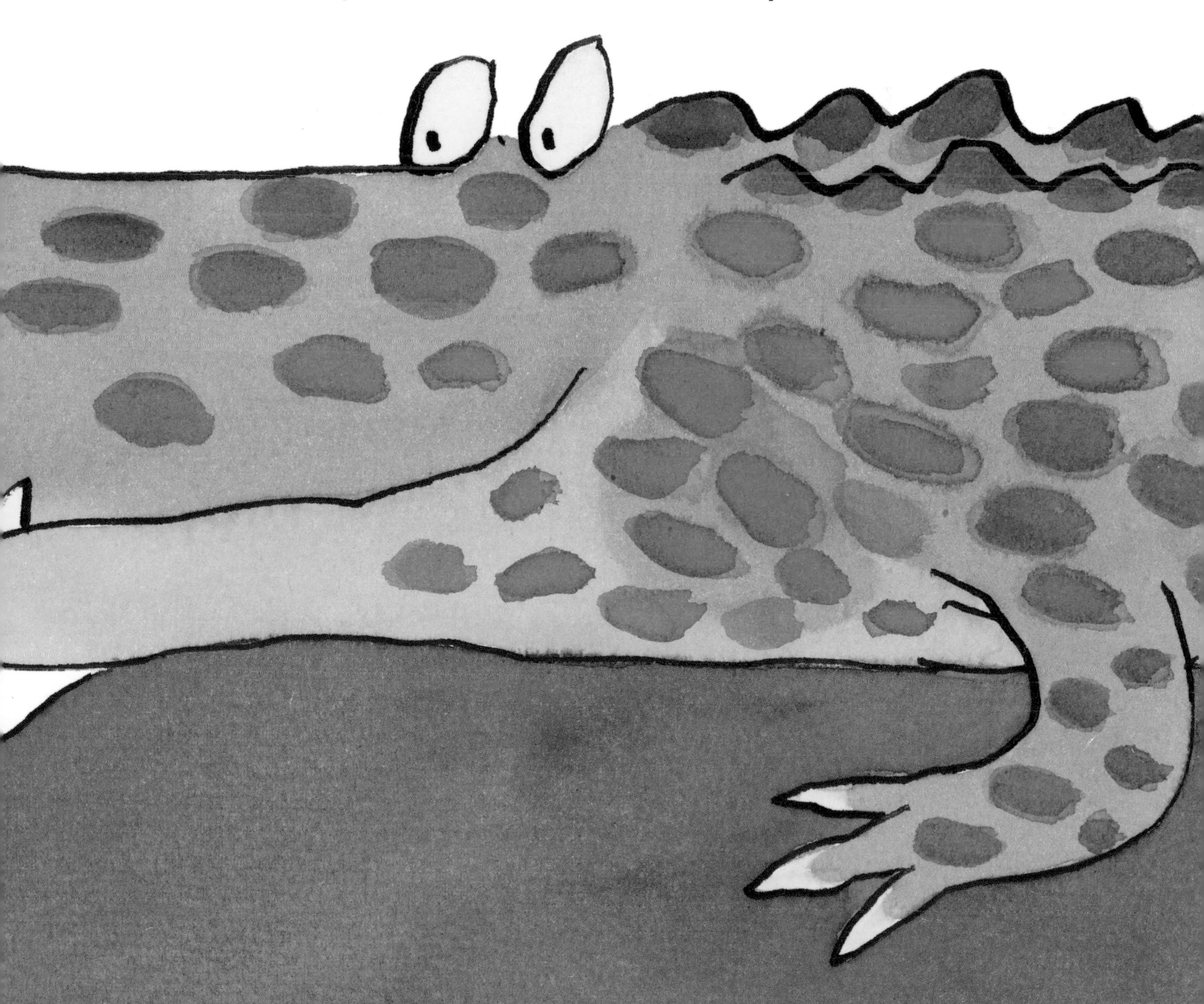

So the strange little creature plodded closer...

and closer . . .

and closer . . .

and just as he was about to climb
onto the crocodile's nose . . .

he heard a voice behind him.

"There you are!"

He turned to see a creature just like him but much, much bigger.

asked the strange little creature.

"I'm your mother," said the big strange creature,
"and you're my little baby chameleon,
the most beautiful and unusual creature in
the whole wide world!
I have been wandering around the jungle,
wondering where you had got to.

Now, come along and meet
your brothers and sisters."

Other books you might enjoy:

9781849394031

9781849393836

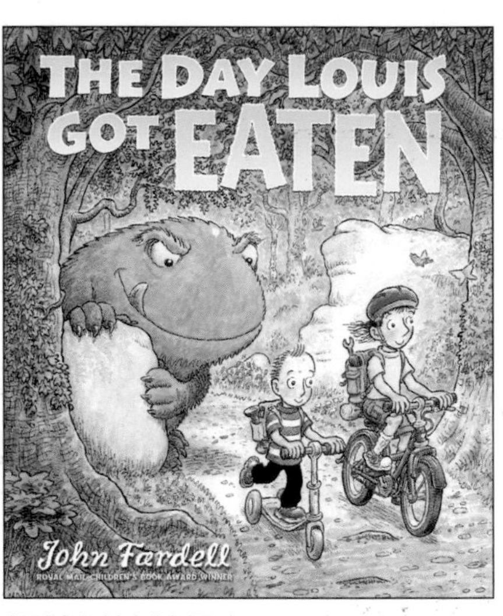

9781849393874

9781849393126

9781849391221

9781849393843